By
Matthew Newman

Edited By
Dr. Howard Schroeder
Professor in Reading and Language Arts
Dept. of Elementary Education
Mankato State University

Produced & Designed By

Baker Street Productions, Ltd.

CRESTWOOD HOUSE
NEW YORK

LIBRARY OF CONGRESS CATALOGING-IN-PUBLICATION DATA

Newman, Matthew.
   Patrick Ewing.

   (SCU-2)
   SUMMARY: Recounts the life story of the young man who came to America from Jamaica, became a basketball star at Georgetown University, and helped the U.S. Olympic basketball team win a gold medal.
   1. Ewing, Patrick Aloysius, 1962-   — Juvenile literature. 2. Basketball players — United States — Biography — Juvenile literature. (1. Ewing, Patrick Aloysius, 1962-   . 2. Basketball players. 3. Blacks — Biography) I. Schroeder, Howard. II. Title. III. Series: Sports Close-ups.
   GV884.E9N48   1986   796.32'3'092'4   (B)   (92)   86-16522
   ISBN 0-89686-315-8

   International Standard   Library of Congress
       Book Number: Catalog Card Number:
       0-89686-315-8   86-16522

PHOTO CREDITS

Cover: Noren Trotman/Sports Chrome
Manny Millan/Sports Illustrated: 4, 16, 19, 41, 45
UPI/Bettmann Newsphotos: 7, 11, 20, 38-39
Heinz Kluetmeier/Sports Illustrated: 8
AP/Wide World Photos: 15, 31, 42, 46-47
Jerry Wachter/Focus On Sports: 23, 28
Focus On Sports: 25, 32
Gill Eppridge/Sports Illustrated: 35, 36-37

Copyright © 1986 by Crestwood House, Macmillan Publishing Company

Macmillan Publishing Company
866 Third Avenue
New York, NY 10022
Collier Macmillan Canada, Inc.

CRESTWOOD HOUSE

Printed in the United States of America
10 9 8 7 6 5 4 3

91-595

TABLE OF CONTENTS

*Patrick Ewing led Georgetown to the NCAA
championship in 1984.*

INTRODUCTION:
A HERO'S HOMECOMING

On October 12, 1984, hundreds of people were gathered around the steps of the city hall in Cambridge, Massachusetts. Citizens from all walks of life — young and old, black and white — had joined in a celebration. It was a special day in their history. One of their own, Patrick Ewing, was coming home.

This homecoming ceremony was the climax of a wonderful year for Ewing. In March, Ewing had led Georgetown University to the NCAA basketball championship. In August, Ewing helped the United States Olympic basketball team bring home the gold medal. Today, Cambridge was honoring Ewing's achievements.

All eyes were on the stage. Patrick Ewing, who had grown up on nearby Pleasant Street, sat in the middle of it all. Sitting next to him was his father, Carl Ewing, along with other family members.

"The city is honored to be where Patrick had his basketball beginnings . . .," Mayor Leonard J. Russel began. "I hereby proclaim October 12th, Pat Ewing Day . . . a great, immortal day in Cambridge. Finally, I present to Patrick Ewing, the key to the city."

Ewing then rose and accepted the key. Afterwards, he was taken to Rindge and Latin High School. He was surrounded by cheering students and old friends. As a student at Rindge and Latin from 1976 to 1980, Ewing had taken the high school basketball team to three state championships.

Mike Jarvis was Ewing's basketball coach at Rindge and Latin. He gave a moving speech about the special nature of Ewing's character.

"Patrick took something God gave all of us — potential. First he discovered it, then he developed it," Jarvis said. "He learned to listen. Once you told him the answer, he never forgot. Not one day of practice did he miss, not even a study hall.

"Nobody received more criticism from the day he started to play. No matter how foolish he looked, how people laughed, he practiced."

Finally, it was Patrick's turn to speak to the audience.

"Well," he began. The words did not come easily. "I really don't know what to say. This brings back memories. I appreciate it, and it feels great to be back home.

"I'm honored to have this day, except that when everyone was talking they made me feel like a saint. Coach John Thompson has said, 'There are no saints in the pivot (middle).' I'd like to thank you for your time and effort."

THE SECOND HOMECOMING

A few months later, Ewing had a second homecoming. This one took place many miles away from America. The site was Ewing's birthplace, Kingston Town, Jamaica.

It had been nine years since Ewing had visited his homeland. He still remembered the crystal blue waters and pure white sands he had played upon as a boy. He

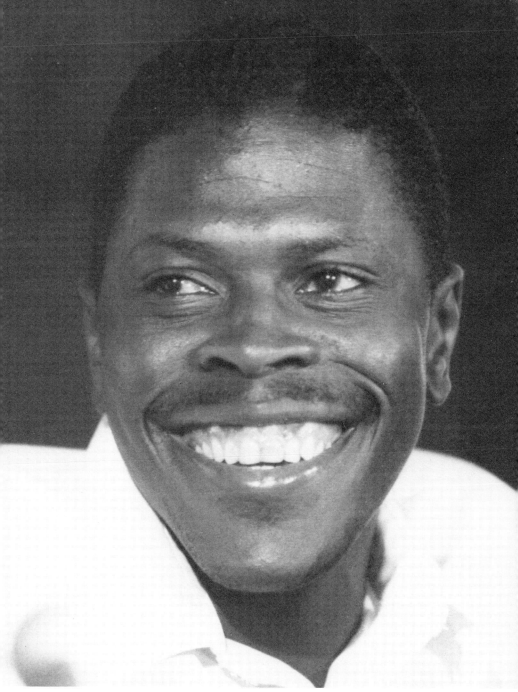

Ewing was born in Kingston Town, Jamaica, in 1962.

also remembered the unpaved streets, crowded shacks, and barefoot children. If Ewing was a hero in America, he was something even greater to his fellow Jamaicans.

As it happened, Ewing's homecoming took place on August 6, 1985, Jamaican Independence Day. It also was Patrick's twenty-third birthday. Along with his father, Ewing listened as Jamaican officials paid him tribute. One official spoke about how Ewing was already being ranked above many of America's top professional basketball players. "He went out and conquered them all," he said. "Jamaica is very proud that we should give birth to such a person."

Ewing charmed the crowd by speaking in the Jamaican accent he hadn't used in years. He also ate several helpings of Jamaican food. In the end, he wanted to leave Jamaicans with more than a brush with a star. He tried to plant seeds of hope.

"I think the best thing I can do is to be an example and present a positive image," Ewing said. "To work hard, play hard, and show them what you can accomplish. There is no easy way."

FROM JAMAICA TO AMERICA

Patrick Aloysius Ewing was born on August 6, 1962, in Kingston Town, Jamaica. Kingston Town is located on the southwestern coast of the island. It is the capital city of Jamaica.

Patrick was the fifth of seven children born to Carl and Dorothy Ewing. Both parents worked to support the family. Although better off than most Jamaicans, the Ewings still lived in the poorest section of Kingston.

Carl and Dorothy had a common dream — they wanted a better life for themselves and their children. They wanted something more than a life in the Jamaican mines for Patrick and the others. For Dorothy Ewing, the key to her dream was education. But education was a luxury few Jamaicans could afford.

In 1971, Dorothy Ewing left Jamaica for the United States. With the help of relatives in New York, she had

Jamaicans were proud of what Patrick had done,
including leading the U.S. team to a gold medal in the
1984 Olympics.

found a job at Massachusetts General Hospital in Cambridge. She quickly became known as a hard worker. She saw her job as a privilege, rather than a duty.

When she left Jamaica, she had promised to send for Carl and the children as soon as possible. Slowly, by ones and twos, they joined her in Cambridge. Patrick arrived on January 11, 1975. He was thirteen at the time.

For Dorothy Ewing, Patrick's arrival in America fulfilled a lifelong dream. "She told us America is the land of opportunity," Patrick said.

PATRICK EWING DISCOVERS BASKETBALL

At age thirteen, Patrick was already six feet tall. He was very slim and athletic. In Jamaica, he had been a soccer goalie. Basketball wasn't very popular there. In fact, before arriving in Cambridge, Ewing had never seen a basketball!

As he walked home from school every day in Cambridge, Patrick used to watch kids play basketball in Hoyt Park. For a long time, he simply watched from a distance. Then, one day, he decided to give it a try himself.

"Hey, do you want to play?" one of the kids asked.

"Sure," Patrick said.

Even with his height, Ewing didn't take to the game quickly.

"I'd watched and seen that the object was to put the ball

It may be hard to believe, but Patrick had to work very hard to learn how to play basketball.

in the basket," Ewing remembers. "It was more difficult than I imagined."

Ewing began to spend more and more time on the court. In the seventh grade, he made his first "slam-dunk." By eighth grade, Ewing had grown to 6'6", and people were starting to take notice. The following year he became the starting center at Rindge and Latin High School.

In more ways than one, things weren't easy for Ewing. Aside from still being a stranger in town, he was still very much new to America. The culture was totally different. He had trouble reading English at the same pace as his classmates. He was shy, but still very noticeable because of his size. He stood out just when he was trying to fit in.

As with all teenagers, Ewing was teased about different things. In Patrick's case, however, his size and background made him an even bigger target for abuse. When Rindge and Latin went to other team's gyms, students sometimes yelled unkind things from the stands.

"I tried to tell him that some of the things that happened on the road, and some of the things said, were all part of the game," coach Mike Jarvis recalls. "People were just trying to get on his nerves. His mother told him — I heard her say this — 'Work hard and do it right or don't do it at all. Let people say or think what they will.' I think Patrick heard his mother much more clearly than me."

THE EWING COMMITTEE

As a sophomore, Ewing was already one of the top high school basketball players in the country. When Rindge and Latin played Boston Latin for the Massachusetts state title, college coaches from across the nation came to watch.

The title game was held at the Boston Garden in Boston, Massachusetts. This is where the Boston Celtics play. John Thompson, who coached at Georgetown University in Washington, D.C., happened to be in the Celtics' offices that day. He hadn't come to see Ewing. Rather, he was just visiting with the Celtics' President, Red Auerbach.

"You've got to see this one kid," Auerbach told Thompson. They arrived at the Garden just in time to see Ewing draw a charge from an opposing player. A while later, Ewing stole a pass, sprinted the length of the court, and stuffed it. Thompson was impressed.

"That was when I said, 'Get me him, and I'll win the National Championship,' " he recalls.

By the time Ewing graduated from Rindge and Latin, he was the most sought-after player in America. Of the ninety-nine games Ewing had played for Rindge and Latin, his team had lost only five. Nearly everyone agreed that Ewing was a 'can't miss' college prospect.

In 1980, a group of concerned Cambridge citizens formed a committee on Ewing's behalf. Their purpose was to try to help Ewing and his parents choose the best college available. The 'Ewing Committee' sent out a letter to 150 different colleges. The letter stated that Ewing might need special help. It asked that Ewing receive tutoring, and be allowed to take untimed tests.

Some people thought the committee made a mistake by sending this letter. Instead of helping him, they thought it made Ewing look like a slow learner.

As word of the letter got around, Ewing was teased

more than ever. Signs were posted at games which said, "Ewing Kant Read Dis."

In fact, Ewing was an above average student. Those close to him spoke highly of his intelligence and effort. Ewing, however, refused to waste his energy by fighting the slurs.

"I don't want to fight it on that level," Ewing said. "I guess I did care about it to a certain degree. But I wasn't going to go around talking about it or let it affect the way I play. As long as my family and friends knew the truth about me, that was all that was necessary. It might have been tough to hear and see that stuff, but I had all the support I needed."

In a way, Ewing's silence said more about his intelligence than any amount of tough talk could have.

EWING CHOOSES GEORGETOWN UNIVERSITY

On February 2, 1981, John Thompson paid a visit to the Ewing home. Thompson, at 6′10″ and three-hundred pounds, was not unlike Ewing. He had also been a highly recruited player years before. He hoped to convince the Ewings that Georgetown University was the right school for Patrick to attend.

Thompson knew that Dorothy Ewing wanted a first-rate education for her son. Still, Thompson disagreed

Mrs. Ewing wanted her son to have a good education.
Together, they selected Georgetown University.

15

with the terms of the "Ewing Letter." He argued that Patrick would do fine at Georgetown without any special assistance. "Don't send your son to us to be educated and then tell us how to educate him," Thompson said.

Mrs. Ewing was impressed by Thompson's honesty. She sensed that Thompson would look out for Patrick's educational interests as well as his basketball skills. She agreed to let Patrick go to Georgetown.

"If I had gone somewhere else, I might have been exploited," Patrick said later. "Coach Thompson is like a father to me, more than just a coach. I think he understands me, and there is no question in my mind that he's the best coach in the world for me. I have never regretted my decision to come to Georgetown, because of Coach Thompson."

THE HOYAS BECOME INSTANT CONTENDERS

As the new center for the Georgetown Hoyas, Ewing found himself in the middle of things in more ways than one. He had gone from the quiet life in Cambridge to the nation's capital. He was the most visible student among thousands on the Georgetown campus. And, he was the focus of sportswriters all across the country.

At first, Ewing was a little shocked by it all.

"I remember calling home a lot and needing my family to cheer me up," Ewing says.

Before Ewing, the Hoyas were not a great team. With Ewing, people expected this to change. At the beginning of Ewing's first year, however, the Hoyas struggled. They lost two of their first three games. The team hadn't found its "chemistry" yet. Patrick and his teammates barely knew each other, on or off the court.

"When he first got here, he was shy," one teammate said. "Even with us, I think he was cautious. After a while, he became comfortable. Patrick is not a naturally out-going person. I think you have to prove to him that you're okay."

Ewing sometimes showed the strain of the pressure he felt. In a game against Nevada-Las Vegas, Ewing stumbled over his own two feet — almost falling flat on his face — during the pre-game introductions.

Before long, Ewing found his footing. The Hoyas streaked to six wins in a row. Ewing's teammates learned

Coach Thompson (center), was like a father to Ewing and his other players.

that Patrick had a presence, one that made the whole team play better. "Just having him standing there creates problems," teammates Sleepy Floyd said. "We can see the other team concentrating on Patrick, and that makes it easier for the rest of us."

Sportswriters began to rank the Hoyas among the top teams in the country. On the court, Ewing was proving to be everything people expected. Off the court, however, things were not going so smoothly. Some people continued to make an issue of the "Ewing Letter." Ugly signs continued to pop up in arenas across the country.

"I don't understand why people who have never met me, or don't know anything about me, say I'm dumb. I'm not dumb," Ewing said.

Another issue that was making headlines was Ewing's physical style on the court. After having a few fights with opposing players, Ewing began to be tagged as a "dirty player." Coach Thompson stood up for his star pupil.

"Pat is not a dirty player," Thompson said. "In our society people are afraid of any tall, black man who plays tough . . . If you talked one-on-one with him, you'd find a gentle, nice, polite kid."

One reason that Ewing got "bad press" was that he did little to overcome it. Thompson asked his players to focus on their studies, rather than on talking to reporters. During games on the road, the Hoyas were often kept away from the press right up until game time. Some said Thompson shielded his players too much. Thompson

Coach Thompson always stood up for his players' best interests.

didn't really care what they said. He was sure he was looking out for the players' best interests.

No one could argue with the Hoyas' results. In his very first season, Ewing led Georgetown to the finals of the National Collegiate Athletics Association (NCAA) Tournament.

In the title game, the Hoyas faced North Carolina. For many watching on television, it was the first chance to see the 7 foot, 240-pound Ewing in action. True to expectations, Ewing did not disappoint them. In the opening eight minutes of the game, Ewing did not allow a single

19

Patrick Ewing defends against North Carolina's Michael Jordan in the 1982 NCAA Championship game.

North Carolina shot to go through the net. In this time span, Ewing blocked each of the Tar Heels' first four shot attempts. In all, Ewing scored twenty-three points and had ten rebounds. Though the Hoyas lost, 63-62, the Ewing Era had begun in a big way.

SAMPSON MEETS GOLIATH

As a freshman, Ewing's efforts as a student were just as important as those on the basketball court. He had a solid "B" average. He found that he loved drawing, and he was majoring in fine arts. During the summer, he applied for a job in the United States Senate. He was accepted as an aide to Senator Robert Dole.

Many said Ewing could have earned $1 million (US) a year as a pro if he decided to quit school early. Instead, he returned to Georgetown for his sophomore season. As it turned out, Ewing again took the Hoyas into the NCAA play-offs. This time, however, the Hoyas were eliminated before the final round.

One of the highlights of the year took place on December 11, 1982. The Hoyas faced the Virginia Cavaliers in a game at the Capital Centre in Landover, Maryland.

The Hoyas and the Cavaliers were two of the best teams in America at the time. Both teams were led by big centers. Ralph Sampson, the 7'4" center for Virginia, had never faced Ewing before. Many thought Ewing and Sampson were the two best players in the country.

"I suppose we are making history," John Thompson said. "This game will have Ralph and Patrick frozen in time."

Some said it was "Sampson versus Goliath." What made the match-up so interesting was the two players' different styles. Sampson was a smooth, graceful scorer who didn't care for too much bumping. Ewing was an "in-your-face" type of player who loved to "mix it up."

As it turned out, Virginia beat Georgetown by the score of 68-63. But Ewing had held his own against Sampson, who was a senior. Ewing scored sixteen points in the game.

THE BIG EAST'S PRINCE OF PERIL

Ever since he came to Georgetown, Patrick Ewing had been labeled as a "bully." For a while, it seemed to go away when Ewing was a sophomore. But as a junior, Ewing got into a few fights and writers began picking up the "bully" theme again. One labeled the Hoyas as "Grandmaster Flash and the Furious Twelve." Ewing himself was called the Big East Conference's "Prince of Peril."

These labels were not meant to be nice. Coach Thompson took them as insults. To some degree, the Hoyas' tactics got more attention than their talent.

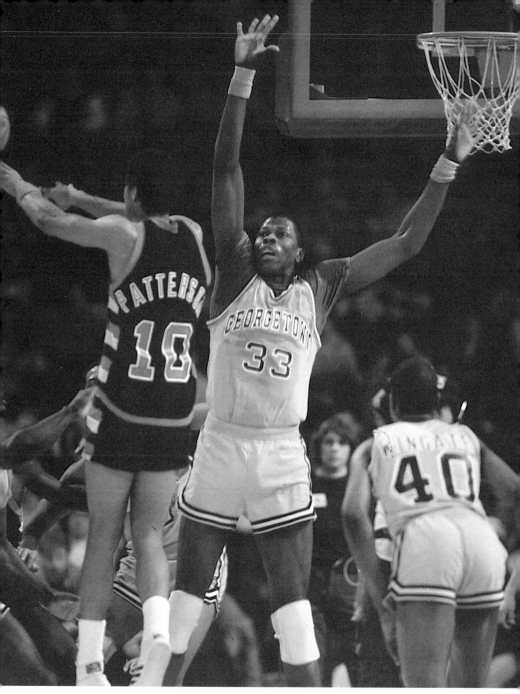

*Ewing was called the "Prince of Peril" for his physical
style of playing.*

For his part, Ewing didn't want to make enemies, but he didn't care about making friends, either. "Intimidation is part of life, it's part of basketball," he said. "The strong get stronger, and the weak get weaker."

For Ewing, being physical on the court was often simply a matter of self-defense. This was the case in one game against Syracuse University in 1984. Late in the second half, one of the Syracuse players suddenly punched Ewing in the ribs. Dwayne Washington, the 6'2" guard for Syracuse, claimed that Ewing had elbowed him first. After being punched, Ewing swung at Washington. It didn't land. The crowd booed Ewing. They hadn't seen Washington's punch.

"We each had emotional reactions, and that happens in a game like this," Washington said after the game. "We shook hands afterwards. What did we say? The handshake did the talking."

As usual, Ewing refused to get caught up in the media "hoop-la" at the press conference following the game. "What fight? What booing?" Ewing said, smiling. "It's over with, and I don't wish to get into anything about it."

THE NUMBER ONE TEAM IN THE NATION

No matter what people said, few denied that the Hoyas were a great team in 1984. Coming into the NCAA playoffs, the Hoyas' record was 29-3. Their three losses had

*The 1984 Hoyas, led by Patrick, had proved they were
a great team.*

been by a total of less than eight points. The Hoyas' defense had held opponents to only 39% shooting, an all-time NCAA record-low.

Ewing was averaging four blocked shots a game. He had said "in-your-face" by blocking over one hundred shots during the season. He also had 371 rebounds and was averaging 16.6 points a game.

In the post-season NCAA Tournament, Georgetown continued to mow down their opponents. And in each game, Ewing played a big role. In the first round, Georgetown faced Southern Methodist University. SMU's stall tactics kept the game close right up until the end. Ewing's tip-in with fifty-one seconds left won it for Georgetown, 37-36.

In the next rounds of the tournament, Georgetown beat Nevada-Las Vegas and Dayton. This set up a showdown between Georgetown and Kentucky.

In the first half against Kentucky, Ewing picked up three quick fouls. When this happened, the Wildcats thought it would be much easier to win, since Ewing had to sit on the bench. But the Hoyas proved they were tough even without Ewing on the court all the time. They held the lead until Ewing returned in the second half. At that point, the Wildcats went to pieces. With Ewing guarding the basket, Kentucky missed twenty-one straight shots. They made only one basket in the final twenty minutes of play. Georgetown won easily, 53-40.

In the Championship Game, Georgetown faced the University of Houston. The Cougars had a record of 32-4.

They were led by a 6'10" center from Nigeria named Akeem "The Dream" Olajuwon. During the NCAA play-offs, "The Dream" was averaging over twenty points a game. Just as Ewing had done for Georgetown, Olajuwon had turned Houston into a national powerhouse.

As the title game began, all signs pointed to Houston being the victor. The Cougars made seven straight long range bombs. They jumped out to a 14-6 lead.

Before long, however, the Cougars began feeling the heat of Georgetown's tight defense. The Hoyas scored a rash of baskets to tie the score at sixteen apiece.

At this point, one of the Cougars took a shot and missed. Olajuwon got the rebound three feet from the basket. At that range, it was usually an easy "two" for Akeem. But this time, Ewing was standing in his path.

Instead of going straight up, Olajuwon head-faked. Ewing stayed on his feet. Olajuwon then went up, but was forced to change his shot and missed. Moments later, Ewing beat Olajuwon to a rebound and scored. From that point on, the Hoyas never trailed.

Three times Olajuwon went up with Ewing, eager to get a block. Each time, Ewing got Olajuwon off his feet and dished the ball off to a teammate for an easy score.

The final score was 84-75, in favor of Georgetown. Ewing scored 10 points and had 9 rebounds. Olajuwon had 15 points and 9 rebounds. Beyond the statistics, Ewing had made his whole team play better. Olajuwon had not. That was the difference between winning and losing.

Ewing helped Georgetown win its first men's basketball crown.

The victory gave Georgetown University its first men's basketball crown ever. And John Thompson became the first black Division I basketball coach to bring home a national title.

For Patrick Ewing, the victory did more than anything else to make him the top college center since Lew Alcindor (Kareem Abdul-Jabbar) in 1969. After the season, Ewing was honored as the Big East Player of the Year. He was also named as an all-American for the second straight season.

EWING JOINS THE UNITED STATES' OLYMPIC BASKETBALL TEAM

In April of 1984, Patrick Ewing once again found himself on the basketball court. Tired as he was from the NCAA play-offs, he had a goal that made him reach down for a little extra — trying out for the United States' Olympic basketball team.

"This is something I've always wanted to do — make the Olympic team," Ewing said. "It's been one of my goals for a long time. Hopefully, it will come true . . . The hardest thing I've done was to win the National Championship. Making the Olympic team would be right up there."

Ewing not only made the team, he started five of the six

contests they played in the Summer Games in Los Angeles.

In a game against Uruguay, Ewing showed why he had been chosen for the team. Uruguay had won the opening tip. A guard went up from deep in the corner for a jump shot. He thought he was far enough from Ewing to get it off. He wasn't.

"He blocked that shot and the ball knocked over a chair in the stands," teammate Jon Konkak recalls. "I sat there going 'Jimminy Cricket.' That play makes you scared. He had a couple of them 'skip-hop-tomahawk' dunks, too. That's got to affect you. Especially those guys (from Uruguay)."

In the end, Ewing was a major reason the United States won the gold medal.

THE HOYAS DEFEND THEIR TITLE

By the start of his senior year at Georgetown, Patrick Ewing had matured a great deal. He knew what his goals were and how he wanted to meet them.

Over the summer, Ewing's value as a pro prospect had soared higher than ever. Still, Ewing knew he had unfinished business at Georgetown. "Graduation and another National Championship are equally important," he said. "I have depended on family, and friends, and Coach Thompson. Now I feel I have moved on. I have learned a great deal. I'm capable of taking care of my own life."

Patrick and the Hoyas beat St. John's on their way to the 1985 finals.

Ewing knew that he and his Hoya teammates had a chance to make history. No team had been able to win back-to-back NCAA titles in twelve years. If the Hoyas won the crown again, they would become only one of six teams ever to do it.

With Ewing at the helm, Georgetown breezed through

Going into the play-offs, the Hoyas had lost only two games.

the regular season. Going into the NCAA play-offs, some people said the Hoyas might be one of the greatest teams ever. For the third time in four years, Georgetown made it into the Championship game. Their record was 35-2. They had seventeen straight wins.

In the NCAA title game, the Hoyas were heavily favored over Villanova. The Wildcats didn't have a player who stood out for them like Ewing did for the Hoyas. Their record was only 25-10. Besides, they had already been whipped by Georgetown earlier in the year.

Still, Villanova was on a roll coming into the NCAA final. Even without a star player, they were playing well as a team. They were coming together just when it counted the most. Some said they were a 'Cinderella' team — a team of destiny.

The game was played before millions of fans watching on television. Ewing controlled the opening tip-off. The ball, however, was batted out of bounds. Moments later, Harold Pressley of Villanova drove the lane and lifted a shot over Ewing. The tone seemed to be set — an upset was in the making.

Throughout the first half, Georgetown fought from behind. Ewing found himself hounded by two or three defenders at all times. Villanova was in control of the game's tempo. Still, everyone expected the Hoyas to explode at any moment.

In the second half, the lead changed hands nine times. With less than five minutes to play, the Hoyas had the lead, 54-53.

At this point, however, the Wildcats surprised everyone by not falling apart. In the end, they managed to pull out a 66-64 victory.

The Hoyas showed a lot of class in defeat. After the final buzzer, they clapped as Villanova fans danced on the floor in celebration. Afterwards, Coach Thompson told the press how he felt about his team's effort.

"I don't want them to hang their heads, run around and cry and make excuses," he said. "We know how to win, and now we have to know how to lose."

The loss ended the Ewing Era on a sad note. Instead of winning back-to-back titles, Ewing was left with three losses in four title game appearances. Still, Patrick had much to be proud about. His 1311 rebounds made him the number one rebounder in Georgetown history. His 2170 points made him Georgetown's second leading all-time scorer. He could also boast of 493 blocked shots. In all, he averaged 15.3 points and 9.7 rebounds a game over four years.

From 1981 to 1985, Ewing led the Hoyas to 121 victories. They lost only twenty-two games. This was the best record for a college team in almost forty years.

After the season, Ewing was showered with awards one final time. He won the Naismith Award for 1985. He was named Big East Player of the Year for the fourth straight season. He was also given the Adolph Rupp and Kodak awards.

If Ewing had one regret, it was that his mother could

The loss in the title game was a sad ending for Ewing's career at Georgetown.

not be there to share in his achievements. She had died of a heart attack before Ewing's junior year.

"I think about her," Ewing said. "I think about how much I miss her and how much I wish that she was here."

Still, Patrick had fulfilled his promise to his mother. In 1985, he graduated on time from Georgetown University.

In the end, Ewing's impact at Georgetown went far beyond the realm of statistics. His fierce pride had forever changed the school's character. In the words of John Thompson, Ewing was "the period to end all sentences at Georgetown."

Patrick wished that his mother could have shared in his graduation.

36

The New York Knicks had first choice in the college draft and picked Ewing.

In the summer of 1985, the National Basketball Association (NBA) held a lottery to see which team would get

the first choice in the college draft. Some people called it the "Ewing Lottery." As it turned out, the New York Knicks got the first pick. As expected, they named Ewing as their selection.

Later that year, Ewing signed one of the richest sports contracts ever. Over ten years, Ewing would earn $30 million (US). His first year salary — $1.7 million (US) —made him the highest paid rookie in NBA history.

"This is a very significant day in the history of the Knicks," the Knicks' President said. "We're looking forward to many years of winning and championship teams."

Many people said that Ewing would have a huge effect on the NBA. When asked how he would handle the pressure of being a "franchise" player, Ewing smiled and gave a typical answer.

"What pressure's that?" he asked.

All joking aside, Ewing was well aware of people's hopes. No one seemed to care that the Knicks had just had an awful season. Their 1984-85 record was 24-58. Without any help, Ewing was supposed to turn the Knicks into a contender.

Never one to back off from a challenge, Ewing promised to give it his all. "I'm very much looking forward to playing pro-style basketball," he said. "In college sometimes it was five-on-one. But in the NBA it will be nice to be covered by one man."

When the Knicks' exhibition season opened, it became clear that no one — not even a man like Ewing — could turn the Knicks into a good team overnight. The Knicks went into a four-game losing streak. Ewing had seldom lost that many games in a season, let alone in the first two weeks!

In spite of Ewing, the Knicks lost their first four
exhibition games.

Patrick earned Moses Malone's respect, even though Malone outplayed him.

"I don't like losing, and I don't want to get used to it," Ewing said.

On October 26, 1985, the Knicks opened the regular season against the Philadelphia 76ers. Ewing was matched against eleven-year, veteran-center Moses Malone. Malone took the young rookie "to school," scoring 35 points and grabbing 13 rebounds. Still, Ewing earned Malone's respect.

"I felt like an old man in a young man's game," Malone said. "He looked a little tired, but that happens when you have to push people throughout the game. He just has to play his game. There's no more I can say. He's one of my friends. The more experience he has, the better he'll be. Just tell him to keep cool and work hard, and he'll be fine."

EWING GETS INJURED

Ewing got better as the season went on, but the Knicks didn't. They continued to avoid the win column. Still, Hubie Brown, the Knicks' coach, did not blame Ewing.

"Like I keep telling everybody," Brown said, "the man can't do it by himself. Don't ask him to do that."

Brown himself, however, was asking quite a lot of Ewing. Even after suffering a series of injuries, Ewing was being asked to play a lot of minutes. Some said the Knicks were pushing Ewing too hard, too soon.

"If they aren't careful, they could break him," said one player. "I hate to see that happen . . ., because he's so good."

Added another player, "If they keep playing Ewing like that, they're gonna have to get the old guys together at Christmas-time and have a benefit game for him to pay his medical bills. He's too important for that."

Meanwhile, the Knicks continued to pile up losses. Ewing was getting banged up like never before. He suffered injuries to his elbow, ankle, and eye. Finally, after fifty games, he suffered a knee injury. He had to have minor knee surgery and sit out the rest of the season.

PATRICK EWING VERSUS KAREEM ABDUL-JABBAR

One of the few highlights of Ewing's rookie season took place in December, 1985. The Knicks faced the World Champion Los Angeles Lakers in Madison Square Garden. For the first time, Ewing was pitted against the basketball legend, Kareem Abdul-Jabbar. The Knicks hung tough behind Ewing's all-out play. Ewing scored 28 points and had 9 rebounds. Jabbar had 26 points and 8 rebounds. Though the Knicks lost 105-99, Ewing won praise from Jabbar.

"Patrick's going to be an excellent player," Jabbar said. "He's only been in the league two months, and he's already very good."

Ewing was equally impressed with Jabbar. "I think Jabbar is definitely the best center in the game today," he said. "He has so many offensive abilities, so many offensive moves. He can pass, too. It's hard for a team to

Patrick injured his knees and had to sit out the end of his rookie season.

Ewing says that his first year in the league was a great learning experience.

double or triple team him because he hands the ball out so well. He can hit the open man. He does so many things so great."

It is quite likely that someday a rookie center will be saying the same things about Patrick Ewing. Despite missing thirty-two games with injuries, Ewing was named

as the NBA's Rookie of the Year in 1985-86. And clearly, the best is yet to come.

"Like I said before, my first time around the league is a great learning experience," Ewing says. "I'll make a lot of mistakes, but hopefully I won't make them twice."

PATRICK EWING'S PROFESSIONAL RECORDS

New York Knickerbockers
1985-86

Games	Field Goals Made	Field Goals Attempted	Percentage
50	386	814	.474

Free Throws Made	Free Throws Attempted	Percentage
226	306	.739

Rebounds	Assists	Steals	Blocked Shots	Points	Average
451	102	54	103	998	20.0